MASTERS OF THE UNIVERSE ™

DANGEROUS GAMES

by Mark Sufrin
illustrated by Charlie Pietrafeso

A GOLDEN BOOK • NEW YORK
Western Publishing Company, Inc., Racine, Wisconsin 53404

Library of Congress Catalog Card Number: 84-82563.
ISBN 0-307-16014-9   A B C D E F G H I J

After years of war and unrest, Eternia was finally at peace. Skeletor, Lord of Destruction, had been beaten back to his fearful den in Snake Mountain. And the Mystic Wall had once again been sealed to prevent invasion. Eternians began to lower their guard against the forces of evil.

King Randor sought advice from Man-at-Arms, his military expert. "We will be easy prey for Skeletor unless we are strong," said the king.

"I have a plan," said Man-at-Arms. "We will hold an Eterniathlon."

Man-at-Arms continued. "The Eterniathlon is a series of physical and military events held on a course laid out across Eternia. Like the games of old, it will toughen our warriors."

Man-at-Arms went on. "Of course, all of Eternia's best warriors will compete—Prince Adam; my daughter, Teela; Fisto.... But as many as possible should enter, if nothing more than to sharpen their skills. And I am to be chief judge," he concluded.

King Randor said, "If you compete, you might inspire that lazy son of mine. Prince Adam has skill but, alas, no fighting spirit."

Man-at-Arms knew that Prince Adam could change into He-Man—the most powerful man in the universe. And he knew that even the prince himself had strength and skill. But he obeyed King Randor.

While the warriors prepared for the Eterniathlon, Skeletor observed their progress in an image he conjured up in his magic pool. He sneered at it.

"Little do they know," he told his Evil Warriors, "that I've broker the Mystic Seal. While they're playing their silly games, you, trusted ones, will get ready to strike.

"By the time those Eternians realize what's happened, I will have captured the Sorceress and Castle Grayskull—with all its secrets. I will rule Eternia—and not even He-Man himself will be able to unseat me."

On the opening day of the Eterniathlon, all the contestants were lined up, waiting for King Randor to signal the start of the games with the first event—the Battle Marathon.

The warriors were all steeled for action, with determined looks on their faces, except for Prince Adam. He alone was relaxed and grinning, pretending—to Teela's annoyance—that the games were boring nonsense. But he knew his father worried about Eternia's fate, and he had decided he would show the king how strong and clever he could be.

As the days passed, the games went on. Teela had taken an early lead by winning such events as the Tree Scout.

Man-E-Faces, disguised as Prince Adam, captured King Randor and Queen Marlena, winning the Infiltration by Stealth.

With his solid defenses, Man-at-Arms took the medal for Tactics and Strategy.

But then Prince Adam defeated Teela in the Armored-Horse Joust.

He also won the Cross-Country Driving Race.

Prince Adam and Teela both had perfect scores on the Laser Pistol Match. With one event left, they stood even. The Swamp Crossing would decide the Eterniathlon.

The Slough of Despond was a fearsome place with terrible beasts and flesh-eating plants. As Eternian warriors got set to cross it, Skeletor, hidden from view, looked on. He had stocked the swamp with some creatures of his own. With his plan for Castle Grayskull in place, he wanted to make sure that the Heroic Warriors were otherwise engaged.

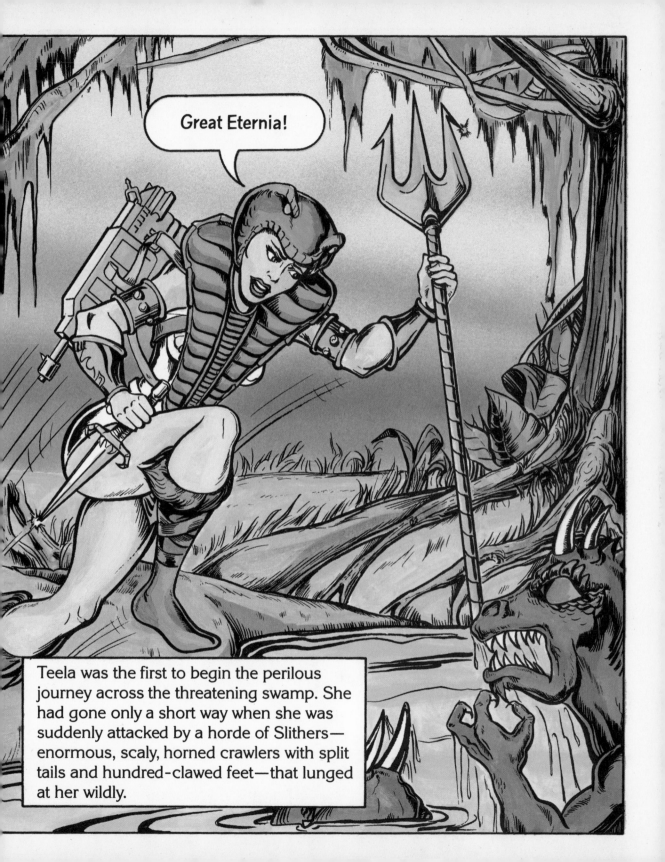

Teela was the first to begin the perilous journey across the threatening swamp. She had gone only a short way when she was suddenly attacked by a horde of Slithers— enormous, scaly, horned crawlers with split tails and hundred-clawed feet—that lunged at her wildly.

Instructing Battle Cat to stay hidden on shore and telling the other warriors to stay back for their own safety, He-Man waded into the swamp. There he joined Teela, who was bravely fighting off the Slithers. Together they sent the monsters back beneath the slime.

As they came ashore, He-Man's keen hearing picked up the faint sound of an overhead vehicle. Looking up, he spotted Skeletor disappearing over the treetops in the Roton.

"So," said He-Man to the other Heroic Warriors, "Skeletor is once more on our doorstep. It is good you have been sharpening your battle skills."

"I wonder what he's up to," said Man-at-Arms.

"No good, I'm sure," said He-Man. "Lead the warriors back to the palace and make sure it's safe. Teela and I will go check things out at Castle Grayskull. I feel uneasy."

Mounting the awaiting Battle Cat, He-Man pulled Teela up behind him.

Teela said, "What about Prince Adam? Even though he ran from the Slithers, I can't just go off and leave him alone in this swamp."

"Don't worry," said He-Man. "I've seen to his safety."

The two warriors started their journey toward Castle Grayskull.

Arriving at Castle Grayskull, He-Man and Teela were shocked to see it surrounded by loathsome beasts. Created by the sorcery of Skeletor and Evil-Lyn, they were being led in their assault by Beast Man.

"I can't understand why the Sorceress didn't warn me about this evil," said He-Man, "unless Skeletor has captured her and is preventing her from reaching me—either in person or by thought."

"We must find out what's happening inside," said Teela.

He-Man, Teela, and Battle Cat, fearless in the face of the beasts, began to charge toward the jaw-bridge entrance to Castle Grayskull. Beast Man's army of creatures was not expecting such a bold attack. They put up little defense as He-Man and Teela, wielding their weapons, broke past them and right into the castle.

Inside Castle Grayskull, Skeletor had used all his magical strength to penetrate the Crystal Chamber that contained the Orb of All Wisdom. Then he had commanded Evil-Lyn to raise the Orb from its underground vault. In another moment, he would capture the secrets of Castle Grayskull and have the power to conquer and rule Eternia.

Evil-Lyn was startled by loud
noises coming from behind her.
Whirling around, she saw groups of
horrible creatures from Beast Man's army
squeezing their way into the room through the
window and two doorways.

"Well," thought Evil-Lyn with glee, "now we have our
chance to defeat He-Man and seize the Orb once
again."

Battle Cat reared up, waiting for the beasts to attack, while He-Man and Teela readied their weapons. They were surprised—but certainly no more so than Skeletor and Evil-Lyn—when the beasts turned instead on the two Evil Warriors.

Skeletor and Evil-Lyn were able to ward off the attack and escape outside, where a confused and frightened Beast Man waited for them in the Roton.

As He-Man and Teela climbed to the top of one of the towers of Castle Grayskull, He-Man said, "I suspect we had some help from the Sorceress. How else would the beasts have turned on their master and his evil cohorts? She is here somewhere in the castle, and I have sent Battle Cat to find her. But meanwhile, we have to settle a score with Skeletor and his crew."

Beast Man spotted the Talon Fighter giving chase. With him and Evil-Lyn looking back, Skeletor flipped a switch on the Roton and sent a thunderstorm toward He-Man and Teela.

The air here is rather dry, don't you think?

"Hold on!" shouted He-Man to Teela as they gained on the Roton. With a quick, skillful maneuver, He-Man bumped the Roton off course…

…and it spun into a black void that was the Lost Corridors of Time.

Later, as He-Man landed the Talon Fighter near the Palace of Eternia, Teela said to him, "Is Skeletor gone forever?"

"I only know that he is gone for now," He-Man answered. "But we must never underestimate the power of evil."

"Will you come to the palace with me to celebrate the victory?" asked Teela.

"No," said He-Man. "I must return to Castle Grayskull and find the Sorceress." Then he smiled and waved good-by to Teela.

At the Palace of Eternia, Teela related all that had happened.

"We are glad you have returned safely, daughter," said Man-at-Arms. "Prince Adam, too, has just returned, finally, from the swamp."

"Once again," added King Randor, "it seems that my son ran from danger—instead of helping you fight off those dreadful Slithers. So we are awarding you, Teela, the medal as winner of the Eterniathlon. However, it will take more than a medal to reward you and He-Man for ridding us of the evil Skeletor."

Man-at-Arms, who knew Prince Adam's secret identity, smiled to himself.

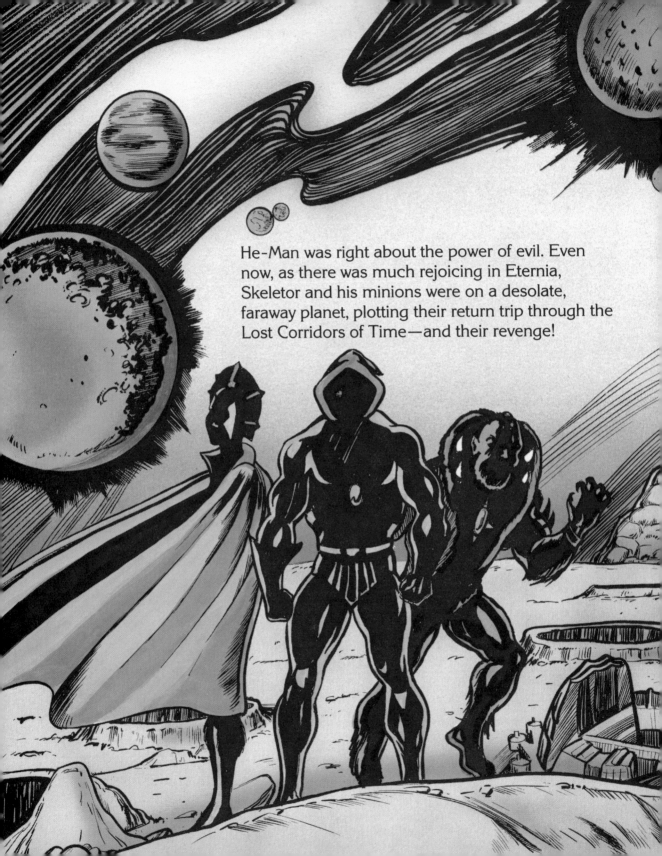

He-Man was right about the power of evil. Even now, as there was much rejoicing in Eternia, Skeletor and his minions were on a desolate, faraway planet, plotting their return trip through the Lost Corridors of Time—and their revenge!